Swan Boy

White Wolves Series Consultant: Sue Ellis,
Centre for Literacy in Primary Education

This book can be used in the White Wolves Guided Reading
programme with more experienced readers at Year 4 level.

First published 2004 by
A & C Black Publishers Ltd
37 Soho Square, London, W1D 3QZ

www.acblack.com

Text copyright © 2004 Diana Hendry
Illustrations copyright © 2004 Jim Eldridge

The rights of Diana Hendry and Jim Eldridge to be identified
as author and illustrator of this work respectively have been
asserted by them in accordance with the Copyrights,
Designs and Patents Act 1988.

ISBN 0-7136-6841-5

A CIP catalogue for this book is available from the British Library.

A&C Black uses paper produced with elemental chlorine-free
pulp, harvested from managed sustained forests.

Printed and bound in Spain by G. Z. Printek, Bilbao.

Swan Boy

by Diana Hendry

illustrated by Jim Eldridge

A & C Black • London

For Cameron Pow – instead of a magic carpet – with love from your story-mother

Contents

Chapter One
Six Brothers

I can still remember the day I left home. How sad I felt!

As usual, all the children ran after me chanting, "Swan Boy! Swan Boy!" Some of them made swan noises, whooping like Whooper Swans do. Others went "Honk-Honk! Honk-Honk!" like the swans on the palace lake and flapped their arms as if they were wings.

Me, I half ran and half flapped. It makes me look very awkward, I know. But walking isn't easy when you have one arm and one swan's wing. Even now I'm not used to it. The wing is wide and heavy.

I can't keep it still. I think the wing remembers when I was all swan.

It wants to lift me off the ground.
It wants to fly. The rest of me
wants to but can't. Not any more.
Not since the time when the new
Queen put a spell on us – me,
Caleb, and my five brothers –
and turned us all into swans.

9

My sweet sister
Lucy freed us
from the spell.
I can't blame her for
what she did. She
did it out of love
and it took her six long
years of painful, lonely silence.

Lucy wanted her brothers back.
And my brothers – Owen, Rory,
Felix, Caspar and Egbert – all
wanted to be princes again. Not
me! I wanted to stay a swan for
ever and ever.

Perhaps I should say that
Lucy *almost* undid the spell.

My five brothers are princes again,
ordinary boys with two arms and
two legs. Now they are all back in
the palace living happily ever after.

And I suppose I might be there
too, maybe not happily, but at
least I'd be myself again, not what
I am now – part boy, part swan.

I might even have forgotten how wonderful it was being a swan, though I doubt it. One thing is for certain. I could have stayed at home. My father would have accepted me as his son again. My brothers would not have turned away from me, ashamed. The children would have shared jokes with me instead of chasing and mocking me.

How unhappy I thought I was going to be, leaving my father's kingdom, journeying to a strange island and living out the rest of my lonely life without my family. And how strangely it has all turned out.

And none of this would have happened if I hadn't wriggled.

Yes, wriggled. You wouldn't think one wriggle could change your whole life, would you? But it has changed mine.

Let me tell you how it all began.

Chapter Two
The Wicked Queen's Spell

Some years after our mother
died, my father went out hunting
in the forest and got lost. He
wandered all day and half the
night, trying to find his way out.
It was very dark and he was tired
and hungry when he met an old
woman who agreed to show him
the way home if he promised her
one thing.

If he refused, she told
him, he would starve to death in
the forest and the birds would peck
his bones.

What could he do? He made
the promise. The "one thing" the
old woman wanted him to promise
was that he would marry her
daughter.

I've sometimes thought my father a foolish man, proud and all too fond of his soft bed and his fine velvet coats, but he's an honest man. He'd made a promise and he kept it even though his new wife was horribly bossy.

She was forever stamping her
foot about something or other and
telling my father to take off his
boots when he came into the palace
or not to leave his socks on the
bedroom floor. Worst of all, she
hated us – my five brothers and me.

She was jealous of my father's love for us and she saw to it that we had very little to eat, that our clothes were never mended, that we were sent to bed early and not allowed out to play in the palace gardens.

Eventually our father was so worried that he took us all off to his castle in the forest so that we would be safe and looked after.

Every day he visited us there in secret, bringing us clean, warm clothes and special plum puddings he'd had the palace cook prepare.

But was the new Queen pleased to have got us out of the palace, out from under her feet, as she used to say? No! She wasn't. She didn't like the way the King disappeared every afternoon when she wanted him to be sitting at her feet. And so she arranged for a servant to follow him into the forest.

Once she knew where we were she made her plan. She had the palace dressmaker sew six silk shirts. And when they were ready, the Queen herself stitched a magic spell into the sleeve of each shirt – the spell that would turn us all into swans. She brought the shirts to the castle in the forest pretending they were a present from my father, the King.

Almost from that very first
moment when the Queen flung
the white silk shirt over my head
and I felt myself changing from
boy to bird, I loved being a
swan. My five brothers hated it.

They tried to fling
the shirts off.
Egbert – he's
the youngest –
even threw
himself on the
ground, rolling
in the mud and
tearing at the shirt with his fingers,
but it was no use.

As for me, I stood very still.
I could feel my heart throbbing
inside me as my arms slowly
changed to wings and my neck
stretched and stretched and
suddenly I was completely dressed
in soft, white feathers.

Imagine yourself, clothed in the lightest, downy duvet. How warm it was! How comfy! Out of all my brothers I had always been the weakest, clumsiest one in the family. So now, when I felt my wings flex, felt the power of them, felt the whole urge to fly shudder through me, I was happy. Happier than I'd ever been when I was a prince.

All six of us rose up into the air as if we'd been born swans and not sons. Below us we heard the Queen laughing.

"Bye bye, boys!" she called. "If I see you on the river I might throw you some stale buns from the palace!"

Higher and higher we flew, all of us dazed and trying to keep together, though Egbert kept bobbing up and down and Owen (he's the eldest) seemed to be going faster than anyone else.

The Queen was now just a tiny figure hurrying back through the forest and the castle, where my father had hidden us, looked like the toy castle I played with when I was five or so.

But the Queen had forgotten about Lucy. Lucy was not at the castle that day. She had gone to visit our cousins. She was on her way back to the castle when she saw us, the six of us, up in the sky, flying we knew not where. We called to her. At least we called as best we could. It came out as a kind of "Honk! Honk!" And our wings made a throbbing "hompa-hompa" sound.

Lucy looked up. Oh how we honked and honked and honked! Owen tore a feather from his side and it floated down at her feet. Holding the single feather, Lucy hurried back to the castle. She found our boy-clothes scattered about the courtyard. She found a few more feathers. And she spent the rest of the day crying and watching the sky for us, her six swan brothers.

And where were we? How can
I tell you of the delight of flying?
Swooping high above the world,
sometimes over the clouds,
sometimes under them. We saw
countries spread beneath us.
Sometimes we had to push against
the wind.

Sometimes the wind seemed to
carry us onwards.

We were creatures of the air.
How dull it seemed to have just
two legs on which to walk about
the Earth!

Then, joy of joy, we discovered water! To be able to fly was a delight, but to be able to sail dreamily down a river was another. The six of us with our heads held high, our wings neatly folded in so that we became like small white boats.

There was no need to talk, even if we could have done. We moved together. I think we were closer then than we had ever been as brothers. Oh, for me that was a kind of happiness I shall never forget.

Perhaps it would have been easier if we had been able to forget that we had ever been the King's sons. But for ten minutes every night, just at sunset, the spell turned us into our boy selves again.

We landed in the castle grounds. We blew on each other's feathers and the swan skins fell from us like shirts. And then what a moaning and a groaning there was!

"All this endless flapping and flying," cried Caspar, "when I was born to be a prince. Born to ride a fine horse, eat a grand dinner, marry a princess."

"And rivers!" groaned Rory. "Whoever thought there were so many rivers in the world. All I want to do is lie down and sunbathe in the palace gardens."

(I should tell you that Rory has never liked water. Not even bath water!)

But oh how Lucy wept and hugged each of us in turn. We couldn't stay. As soon as the sunset faded and darkness set in, we were swans again. Away and flying high, high over the land, leaving Lucy behind.

But those ten minutes were long enough to tell Lucy about the silk shirts and the wicked Queen's spell. Long enough for my brothers to beg Lucy to help us.

Lucy wandered the forest not knowing what to do and weeping for us, her lost brothers. She wouldn't go back to the palace, though my father, the King, begged her to come home. She couldn't eat. She couldn't sleep.

By the time she met the old woman who told her how to undo the wicked Queen's spell she had grown pale and thin. And, for a girl like Lucy, what the old woman told her to do was the hardest thing in the world!

Chapter Three

Lucy's Story

The old woman told Lucy that
she must pick all the stinging
nettles of the forest with her bare
hands. She must trample on
them with her bare feet and turn
them into flax. She must stitch
six shirts, one for each of us.
And if this wasn't hard enough,
she must not speak, smile,
laugh, cry or sing until she had
finished making all six shirts.

 Sweet Lucy!
She who was
always smiling,
laughing, singing
and most of all
chattering so that
often we called
her Lucy Chatterbox, how sad life
became for her.

My father sent messengers to
every corner of the kingdom
looking for us, but of course he
didn't know we had been turned
into swans. And of course Lucy
couldn't tell him. The messengers
returned without news of us and
my father gave us up for lost.

He couldn't understand why
Lucy wouldn't leave the forest,
why she would do nothing but pick
and trample the nettles.

He tried to make her talk again
by bringing friends who wanted to
gossip with her, princes who
wanted to marry her, but nothing
would stop Lucy from her picking
and trampling and stitching.

Very soon her pretty feet and hands were raw and red. I think she had almost forgotten how to sing and smile.

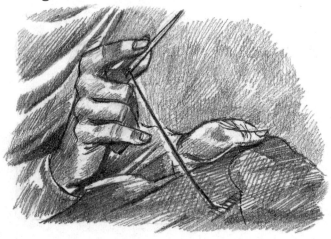

Six long and lonely years went by. And then the Queen came up with another wicked plan. When she discovered what Lucy was doing in the forest, she guessed that Lucy was trying to save us.

"Your daughter has gone mad," she told the King. "Why else does she stay in the forest picking nettles and trampling on them? And why will she not speak? Has she lost her tongue?"

"She is missing her brothers," said the King. "That is why she doesn't speak."

"Ah well," said the cunning Queen. "If she was truly missing her brothers, she would cry. But I've heard that she never cries. Test her! Ask her if she loves you. Ask her three times. If she isn't mad and if, as your daughter, she truly loves you, she will answer."

And so the King and the Queen and a dozen servants rode into the forest. They found Lucy stitching the very last shirt. Oh, how much she wanted to greet the King, to feel his arms around her, to smile and chatter as she'd done in the past. But she kept her head down, stitching, stitching, and said not a word.

"Go on! Ask her!" taunted the Queen.

So three times the King asked her.

"Lucy, my dearest daughter," he said. "I need to hear your voice again. Please tell me – do you love me, your father?"

How could Lucy stop her tears? But she didn't cry and she didn't speak.

Twice more the King asked her and still she only stitched and stitched.

"I told you!" shrieked the Queen. "She's completely mad! Lock her up!"

It was almost sunset and the servants were just about to seize her when we six swans flew towards the castle.

Lucy looked up and saw us.
Hastily she put the last stitch in
the last shirt and just as we were
flying in to land she flung them up
in the air so that as we landed in
the courtyard, the shirts slipped
over our heads.

And now there was no need for us to blow off each other's feathers for that nightly ten minutes when we became boys again. We were about to change back for good.

My brothers stood perfectly still. They held their swans' wings folded close. But me?

As I felt myself changing back, I couldn't bear the thought of being a prince again. Never to beat my grand wings against the wind! Never to fly above the clouds! Never to sail dreamily down a river!

I fought the shirt! I tried to dodge it as it slipped over my head. I tried to flap it away. I wriggled. But the shirt was over me – at least over all of me but for this one wing.

Chapter Four
The Isle of Nanna

Of course my father, the King, was delighted to have his sons back again. It was the wicked Queen who was locked up, not Lucy.

That night we all went back to the palace and had a party. But even then I could see that the King could hardly bear to look at me. My brothers wanted me to hide the wing under a cloak but that was impossible for whenever I moved, the wing flapped.

It wanted to be free. And so did I.

Lucy stroked my wing and
wept. She thought it was her fault
that I was part boy, part swan.
When I told her that I had been
happier as a swan, she simply
wept even more. I think if he could,
my father would have kept me
inside the palace for ever so that
no one could say, "Look! There's
the King's strange son."

As for my brothers, they hated being reminded of the time when we were all swans. They hated it when the children ran after them shouting, "Where's your funny swan brother?" or, "Are you all going to grow wings? When are you going to fly away?"

After a while they would never be seen out with me. I even heard Caspar pretending that I was dead.

Sometimes I would go and sit beside the swans on the palace lake, and wish and wish I could be a swan again. And often I would go back to the castle in the forest where no one could see me.

It was there, in the forest, that I met the old woman who had told Lucy how to undo the magic spell.

"You will never be happy here," she said. "Go to the Isle of Nanna. There they will love you, for the people there have wings in their hearts and wings in their minds."

I had no idea what the old woman meant. How could anyone have wings in their heart or wings in their mind?

But I did what she told me. I took one last look at my old home. I said goodbye to the grand palace set high on the hill and surrounded by a huge wall.

Goodbye to the town huddled around it, the hedged fields and the forest beyond. Then I went down to the harbour and set sail for the Isle of Nanna.

How different the Isle of Nanna was from my own kingdom! Here was a beach of white sand.

Meadows with vines and fruit trees ran up the hills. There were cottages and gardens full of flowers.

And what a welcome I was given! All the children rushed to greet me. They wanted to be tucked under my wing. Every night, at least six of them would sleep beside me under the soft feathers of my swan's wing.

And the Wise Man of the Isle told me why the people here have wings in their hearts and wings in their minds.

"Who has not looked at a bird and wanted to fly?" he said. "But that is not given to people on Earth. But we can send our thoughts flying – flying all over the world. And we can send love flying too. Love, like a swan, can travel miles and miles and miles."

And so I have stayed on the Isle of Nanna, looking after the children. Once a year, on the day of my arrival on the island, we have a special celebration called Swan Day and everyone dresses up in snow-white feathers.

They wanted to give me a palace of my own, but I didn't want it. I have a small house near the sea where I can watch swans flying overhead and where I can be with the children.

And whenever I think of my father, my brothers and my sweet sister Lucy, I try to send love flying too.

I think one day it will reach them. I think one day we will meet again.

About the Author

Diana Hendry has worked as a journalist and a teacher in a boys' school, but is now a full-time writer. She has taught creative writing and still gives workshops in schools and at festivals, and she even spent one year as a writer-in-residence in a hospital in Scotland. For many years she lived in Bristol, but her home is now in Edinburgh.

Diana has written over thirty books for children – from picture books to books for middle readers to a teenage novel. She won the Whitbread Award for *Harvey Angell*. She has also written poetry, radio plays and book reviews.

Other White Wolves titles you might enjoy ...

Hugo and the Long Red Arm
by Rachel Anderson

When Hugo breaks his arm, he thinks he'll be bored and useless. But with his mum's new twisting, grabbing and twirling invention, Hugo's world is turned upside down!

Live the Dream! by Jenny Oldfield

Zoey leads an ordinary life, but her secret wishes are far from normal. When she logs on to the net, she has the chance to make her wildest dreams come true. Which one will she choose?

 **White Wolves**

Detective Dan • Vivian French

Buffalo Bert, the Cowboy Grandad • Michaela Morgan

Treasure at the Boot-fair • Chris Powling

Hugo and the Long Red Arm • Rachel Anderson

Live the Dream! • Jenny Oldfield

Swan Boy • Diana Hendry

For older readers ...

The Path of Finn McCool • Sally Prue

The Barber's Clever Wife • Narinder Dhami

Taliesin • Maggie Pearson

Shock Forest and Other Stories • Margaret Mahy

Sky Ship and Other Stories • Geraldine McCaughrean

Snow Horse and Other Stories • Joan Aiken